Silo 49: Flying Season for the Mis-Recorded

Book Four in the Silo 49 Series

A WOOL Universe Book

Ann Christy

Copyright 2014 Ann Christy.

All rights reserved. No part of this document may be reproduced or transmitted in any form or by any means, electronic, mechanical, photocopying, recording, or otherwise, without prior written permission of the author.

This is a work of fiction. All resemblance to actual persons, living or dead, is entirely coincidental and the product of a fevered imagination.

Cover Art
Torrey Cooney - http://torriecooney.blogspot.com
Formatting
Polgarus Studio - http://polgarusstudio.com

Books In the Silo 49 Series

Silo 49: Going Dark

Silo 49: Deep Dark

Silo 49: Dark Till Dawn

Silo 49: Flying Season for the Mis-Recorded

Contents

Chapter One – Race Year 71 1
Chapter Two 9
Chapter Three – Six Years Earlier 23
Chapter Four 29
Chapter Five 33
Chapter Six – Thirteen Years Earlier 37
Chapter Seven 47
Chapter Eight 51
Chapter Nine 57
Chapter Ten 67
Chapter Eleven 73
Chapter Twelve 77
Chapter Thirteen – Ten Years Later 81
Epilogue – Race Year 89 83

Author's Foreword

You and every other reader of the Silo 49 series took a chance on a totally untried author and made this series a Kindle Bestseller in the genre for Six Months and Counting! For that, I thank you and can't express how much I appreciate you taking that chance.

If this is the first Silo 49 book you've picked up…STOP. This is the third in terms of silo 49 chronology and the fourth in reading order.

The emails I receive are a treasure and filled with really smart questions…and a few requests. Since Silo 49: Dark Till Dawn came out the question I've received most runs a bit like this: Will we ever hear the story of Greg and Lizbet? The second most common question is whether or not I'll write about what happens after Dark Till Dawn. To the first question, this novelette is my answer. I've written it just for you. To the second question I can't give you a yes or no answer. It's a very different story and I'm not sure I can do it justice because it would have to be a very special book indeed.

With many thanks to Hugh Howey for his generous permission to publish this series set in his world of WOOL and the Silos and with affection for my fellow WOOLians, Ann Christy

Chapter One – Race Year 71

Lizbet shoved the last vegetable tray into the freeze drying machine and slammed the door home with a little extra force. The hinges needed to be worked on but until it actually quit shutting reliably, it would remain on the work list. There were always other broken things moving past the not-quite-broken items on the work lists. She hit the buttons that set it to work and listened for the fans and compressor to kick on.

When the buzzing whine seemed stable she turned to inspect her work area. Nothing on the floor, no forgotten trays of cut vegetables, packing tables clear and clean, the knives sharpened and in their sheaths. The vacuum sealer in the corner was cleaned and ready for the next day, its stack of buckets and bags neatly arranged and waiting. She gave a nod of satisfaction then sniffed at her hands and arms. Not too bad today. She was lucky it was carrots and not onions. No amount of scrubbing would get that smell off and she didn't have a lot of time to waste tonight.

At the door she squared her shoulders and made sure her face was without expression, the familiar flush of anticipated embarrassment making a hot spot in the center of her belly. She raised her chin just enough to seem unbothered, but not so much as to seem proud, and opened the door.

Second shift was in full swing in the vegetable processing room and a dozen pairs of eyes followed her as she strode quickly past the people at their long tables full of produce. Knives, cutters and scrapers stilled and she could feel their eyes on her back like little points of pain. Lizbet pushed through the swinging doors and kept walking toward the door that led to the safety of the compartments. Behind her, the voices and noises of work increased once more.

Like always, the pressure eased at about ten paces away and she sucked in a deep breath of relief. One more day gone. Going to and leaving from work were the two worst moments of her day and she counted each one completed without incident a victory. There was no one in the hallway leading to the single compartments so she pulled the kerchief from around her head and let her hair fall free after being confined all day. Her hair actually hurt when she let it fall, a sore tugging on her scalp. The tight binding of her kerchief bent the hairs and the roots protested when the weight came back. It happened at the end of every work day and she'd grown to like the soreness. It was the same kind of pleasant discomfort that came from stretching in the morning after a deep sleep.

Her room was the last in the hallway, with the further space of an empty room between her and the next occupied compartment. Though it was never said specifically, she knew no one wanted to risk sharing a wall with her. Especially not while they slept. She even had her own bathroom so that nothing of hers would touch anyone else's, even obliquely. She didn't mind. She might as well have some benefit from being nearly untouchable.

Inside her room, she stripped the sweaty coveralls off and flung them over the back of her chair. In her tiny shower, she scrubbed her skin till it hurt. She let the water run over her, easing the tight muscles in her arms and using a decadent amount of hot water. Toweling off, she sniffed her arms again and detected the faint dirty sweetness of carrots but she didn't think it was too bad. It was almost nice. Tonight was a big night and she wanted everything to be perfect.

The tunic she had just finished sewing the night before hung from the front of her closet. It was daring and of her own design. It wouldn't just raise eyebrows, it would drop jaws. Dyed the darkest color she could find, it looked purple in the light but black in dim light. Small bright blue spots were sewn around the bottom of the hem in the back, yellow spots on the front. The bottom half was short enough that it barely reached past her shorts and the top half wasn't much of a half at all. Two wide strips of cloth were anchored at the front waistline of the skirt and crossed over her chest, crossed again in back and were then sewn onto the skirt at the sides.

Small orange ribbons kept the crossed bits in place and held all her parts where they should be. She smiled and ran her hands down the supple cloth. It would fly when she moved and her feet tapped in anticipation of the music to come.

She changed into her dancing shorts, ribbons run through the hems at the bottom and tied around her thighs to keep it snug no matter what she did. Today the ribbons were appropriately red. She slipped the tunic on and smiled at her reflection in the bare metal mirror. Perfect.

Pulling the coveralls over the tunic was tricky and she was left with a little bulge around her hips, where the tunic beneath bunched up. It would tell anyone who looked carefully where she was going and what she was up to. Then again, hundreds of other teen shadows would be taking to the stairs in the same state, so that didn't matter much. She shoved her sandals into her satchel, added a quick spray of scent and a smudge of charcoal around the rims of her eyes. She was ready.

There was a shadow in the butterfly garden as she passed by on her way to the landing. It should have been empty by this time. People weren't supposed to muck about in there at all really, but particularly not when it was after regular farm hours and no one was there to monitor them. It was her duty, along with her caster's, to see to the butterflies so, as much as she might like to, she couldn't just pass on by and not do anything. She paused, wondering if she should see who it was or go get Marcus to do it. Depending on who was in there, that person might react badly to her sudden appearance. She saw the shadow move and bend down. Curiosity won out—particularly since the door had been left cracked open—so she peeked in, ready to back away in a hurry should it be someone she couldn't interact with.

Luckily the person was Marcus, the farmer who had sponsored her and acted as her reluctant caster. He was bent over the patch of parsley and looking intently at something within the bundles of curly leaves.

"Something wrong, Marcus?"

He started at the sound of her voice and rose too quickly, stumbling backward. She reached out to catch him but he jerked his arm back before her fingers made contact. She pulled away, expression carefully neutral. Marcus may have sponsored her and he may have been one of the only people who seemed comfortable speaking with her alone, but he was no different than anyone else when it came right down to it.

"I didn't mean to startle you. I was just passing by and saw someone in here," she explained, looking down at a butterfly on the ground near her feet. It was wafting its wings slowly and canted a little to the side. This one wouldn't fly again.

"Ah, don't worry about it, Lizbet. I'm an old man and startle easily. I just came to see them." He waved a hand at the litter of dead and dying butterflies on the plants and ground. "It's getting toward the end of flying season."

She murmured an assent and bent toward the canted butterfly. The larger blue spots among the yellow and black meant this one was a female. She laid a finger on the ground in front of it and felt the tickle of its tiny legs as it crawled up her extended digit. She knew it was silly, but when she did this, she imagined they felt relief to be away from the hard, cold floor. She carefully transferred the weakening creature to the parsley and let her crawl off at her own pace. Only when the butterfly was safely away did she speak. "But flying season will come again for them."

Over the years of her life, Lizbet had become expert at looking at people without actually looking directly at them. She saw Marcus stiffen a little, the posture one that spoke of concern.

She had said it too expressively, she thought. She rose again, gripped her satchel in front of her and lifted her eyes for the barest second to meet his. "They'll be back. Everything that is of us—everything good—is born again to the silo. Nothing is wasted. Not even souls." She gestured at the struggling butterfly and said, "Not even their souls."

They said nothing more for a moment. Lizbet was conscious of each minute passing her by. She really wanted to go but Marcus wouldn't have been here just to see butterflies. He must want to say something to her. The farms were dark for the night, the farmers at home. If he was here it was for a reason. She wondered who had complained about her now.

"Listen, Marcus. I've been doing what I'm supposed to. Keeping to myself…"

He raised a hand to interrupt her. "Oh, Lizbet. It's nothing like that. I…" He stopped and cleared his throat uncomfortably. "I just wanted to wish you a happy birthday. Since you're off tomorrow and everything."

She flushed and tried not to smile. "Oh, thank you. Thank you for remembering."

He shuffled his feet and cleared his throat again. "Well, it's a big one, isn't it?" He pointed at her satchel and the red tag hanging from the strap. "You're going for one last dance?"

Lizbet spun the matching tag around her wrist and said, "One more night and then I age out."

He laughed and said, "I remember that day. Turning twenty felt like the end of the world. Well, now you'll have to settle down like the rest of us." He stopped abruptly, realizing what he had said and how absurd it was. He reached out a hand and came within a hair's breadth of her shoulder, something he had never done before. His gaze fell for the briefest moment on the ridged circle of scar tissue on her cheek, her own personal and permanent 'O' carved in flesh, and his hand fell back to his side.

"You know what I mean," he added quietly.

They both knew there would be no "settling down". There would be only the unending solitude she had now, except that it wouldn't be broken once a fortnight inside the walls of 25 Drums, where all were the same and all were welcome. It would just be this ceaseless shoveling of food into and out of machines and a meal she picked up to eat alone in her room after her shift. And dreams of how it should be different, of course. Always the dreams.

"It will be okay, Lizbet." He knew. He was saying goodbye.

"Yes," she said, her tone as flat as ever. "It *will* be okay."

She looked down again. He was uncomfortable once more. He shuffled to the door of the enclosure, his back bent with age and decades spent over a spade in the soil. "Have fun tonight. I'll see you," he said as he left the enclosure.

When he was gone, Lizbet saw that there were two more butterflies on the ground that wouldn't make it. After six years of shadowing inside the farms she had come to know their motions well. She could tell which ones were resting and who was finished with their duty to life and simply waiting to die.

It was precious time she was using, but she let each crawl to her fingers to be returned to the parsley. They had no expressions—no communication—but they seemed content there. Tomorrow their little bodies would be plucked away but for now, they could be where it was familiar and safe. They could have the company of others like themselves.

The screen door sign read, "Close me!" in emphatic letters. Farmers in the silo were so efficient at their jobs, including harvesting, that these poor creatures had been made almost extinct. Kept here, in their own enclosure with their own plants to put their eggs on, their numbers were sound. But they *were* caged. They fluttered their wings and rested on the screen like bright sparks of color. She could almost feel their inborn desire to get beyond it.

She pulled the door closed behind her and stopped, her hand resting on the handle. It was the end of flying season. There would be more than enough eggs laid by now to ensure another year. She looked around the darkened farm and saw no one, no profile among the plants and no sound of rustling leaves during an evening stroll. The door opened again without a squeak and she strode quickly away without looking back. The current of wind created by her swift departure made for an easy path and wings fluttered in her wake.

Chapter Two

The stairs were nothing to her and the levels passed quickly. She could have easily been a porter or any other profession that required the stairs if anyone would have been able to tolerate her touching their things or knocking at their door for a delivery. Her easy physicality was just something she had been born with, like big eyes or pale skin. She was good at anything that took dexterity or used the body in controlled ways.

When she had danced for her mother as a child, even after what happened, her mother had always been amazed by what Lizbet could do. There were never any scoldings when she leapt from the couch to twirl in the air and then land, light as a cat, all the way across the room. Instead, her mother would clap in delight and then lift her to spin her around in their family's compartment. But that amazement had always been joined by the cautious warning to never show it to anyone else. They wouldn't understand.

She was too much like her father and Lizbet knew it. As she flew the stairs toward the growing sound of drums in the distance she knew that it must be terrible for the families of the women her father had hurt to see her on the stairs, never knowing when it might happen and therefore, never prepared for the sight. She was the very image of him in female form, the same loose curls that had made her father seem so harmless, the same large eyes of a color so dark brown they were almost black, the same heart shaped face and pointed chin. How could nine motherless children and six widowed men overlook her when they might see her anywhere or anytime?

She understood their aversion. What she couldn't understand was the cruelty.

The beat of the drums grew more distinct. Sounds of laughter on the landing still a few levels away spurred Lizbet on faster, her heart beating heavy in her chest as the rhythm of the drums resolved into a recognizable tune. Skipping lightly onto every third step, she had to hold the central post to keep from flying over the rail as she went faster and faster. At the landing she leapt off and shuffle skipped to a stop just shy of hitting the wall. The crowd at the entrance was dwindling as they were let into the club but there were still more people than she was comfortable with mingling in groups on the landing.

This was a sort of danger zone for Lizbet and it was worse because it was an unpredictable danger. Some nights the landing would be just an extension of 25 Drums itself, with kids mingling and dancing, though a much more discreet sort of dancing than that which went on inside. On those nights she was just another dancer.

On other nights they were still firmly fixed into their roles within the silo. Those nights were hard. They turned from her and avoided her eyes or muttered words like *'Other'* or *'Mis-recorded'* under their breaths out on the landing. Inside, they dropped those faces and danced with abandon, even going so far as exchanging a word with her now and then.

Those nights were difficult not because of what they did before they went inside. They were hard because they could drop those faces so easily and let it go once inside. Lizbet never could. No matter what happened within 25 Drums, if she were to meet any of them the next day and put out a hand in greeting, they would shrink from her in horror or embarrassment. She was, and would always be, the half-Other pariah. She would always be the only child ever born in the silo to an Other, a creature that only looked human but had none of the redeeming qualities of a human. A killer of humans.

Tonight it wasn't so bad on the landing. No one even looked at her, really. This year all three racers were under twenty years old and all three had shown up for 25 Drums according to what she heard as she approached. That would include the little wallflower she had never quite taught to dance, the only person she could call friend. It had everyone a twitter since one of the racers was a girl and two were boys. *Something for every*one, Lizbet thought wryly.

She breezed past the assembled crowd toward the lift station. The big fabric bucket was shipped for the night, sagging and empty on the platform over the yawning depths of the silo below. She pulled the bucket off the platform and pushed it to the side. Stepping onto the platform, she lifted the gate latch that kept the bucket from falling should anything unbalance it. She swung it wide and leaned over the gap to catch the breeze that always ran up the silo. It didn't let her down tonight, blowing the ends of her hair and cooling the sweat that beaded her face from her quick trip on the stairs. When she felt cool again—cool enough that she shivered—she stepped back and latched the gate.

At the door she showed her apprentice badge and gave her name. The doorman gave her a look after he checked the list and asked if she wanted to be Drummed Out for her last night. She just shook her head and moved past him before anyone else heard what he was saying. The last thing she wanted was a public reminder of anything, let alone her last night here.

She ducked into the girls changing area and stripped off her coveralls, earning a few gasps at her new wardrobe style. Here there was no need to hide her eyes or keep her hands tightly to her sides, no need to try to seem small or invisible. Here the looks were often admiring, if discreetly so. She slipped off her boots and wound her sandals around her legs tightly for the work ahead. Lizbet tried not to smile in victory as the girls around her looked with sidelong glances at how her outfit had been put together or touched their own clothes with regret. It wasn't nice, but there were so few ways for her to be worth anyone's consideration—even if that attention was just because of her clothes—she couldn't help but enjoy it.

The clerk at the bag-check took her bag and she waited long enough to see which cubby her bag went into out of habit. If one left early it could take forever for the clerk to find the matching tag to the one on a wrist. She ripped a quick salute at the clerk, who was older and only ever frowned back, then pushed through the thick curtains that enclosed 25 Drums.

The heat of so many bodies, the dizzying mix of flashing red lights and the deep pressing sound of the drums engulfed her. As it did every time, the combination pulled her out and away from herself, making her worries and her past disappear like vapor. Lizbet closed her eyes, raised her arms and let her body carry her forward however it wanted. Inside the crush of bouncing, pulsing and dancing young people she let herself go. Other dancers created a gap in their groups when they noticed who she was, but there was none of the jerking away in avoidance she sometimes dealt with. Eyes watched her, sometimes subtly but most of the time not so subtly.

She wasn't stupid enough to think it was really her that they watched. It was the Other-blood they thought she had running in her veins. That hint of danger and wonder at what she might do. That her bones seemed to bend and flow as she moved around the floor didn't dispel that notion. If anything, it made them whisper that it was proof of her Otherness. After all, Others only looked human and had no souls. The Others obeyed the urges of the body and it was their endless hungers that had destroyed the world and trapped humanity in the silo in the first place. Had she been ugly or plain and danced like a wooden stick they would have found a way to make that proof of Otherness, too. There was no winning in this matter.

She pulled her mind back from the music with some difficulty in order to take in her surroundings. Everyone appeared to be here and in their places. Near the center danced the Mechanical boys with their cocksure grins, sly smiles and tousled hair. It was a good spot to be seen from and that was always the aim of the bad boys of Mechanical with their broad shoulders and strong arms.

Near them—at a distance almost as precise as the ticking of a clock—danced a tight little huddle of Water Girls. With their complicated braids and vague scent of chlorine, there was no way to miss them and that was exactly as they wanted it. Blue, the color of water pipes, was their signature and this year they were staining a streak on each cheek with blue dye as well as the centers of their lips. It looked better than what they had been doing a few years back, creating a wide swath of blue dye that ran across their eyes and temples like a mask. They were so alike in their prettiness and they giggled whenever a Mechanical boy swayed their way or looked at them with heavy lidded eyes.

Near the edge of the dance floor where the best lighting was, the farmer boys and girls postured eloquently to the pounding music, showing their lamp browned skins to best effect. They always wore the smallest possible amount of clothing and rumor had it they hid within the fields to baste themselves under the lamps without their clothes on. Given the tiny nature of the shorts she was seeing and the uninterrupted expanses of deliciously browned skin, she believed it. She had never dared to search out the spots they used in the farms to do this, but the temptation to strip down and baste herself like they did had always been a strong one.

Here in 25 Drums serious IT girls met silly Service boys, studious Supply boys met fun-loving Porter girls and everything in between. There was no Up-Top, no Mids and no Down Deep in 25 Drums.

In this place the whole of the silo youth met and mingled. As long as you were a shadow, unmatched and under the age of twenty, you were welcome. Matches were made here between people that would never have met otherwise and that was just as it was supposed to be. Mix, mingle and find a mate.

Losing the bazaar and theater to drums and flashing lights every two weeks was a small price to pay for the benefits. Lizbet might not make a match here, but she was never turned away. The rules were simple: no fighting and leave your problems at the door. Here it was all about the dancing and the heated blood of healthy young people in high spirits.

She felt eyes on her back and turned to find her wallflower exactly where he always was. He winked and smiled when she met his eyes and she threw back her head and laughed. No longer just her wallflower—hopelessly wooden no matter the dance and about as rhythmic as a fully laden bumblebee—he was now her Racer wallflower. The blue, red and white of his coveralls advertised his new status from all the way across the dance floor.

She made her way over to him and grinned at his false discomfort when she swung her hips and took the last two steps. "Think you can do that yet? Maybe your new outfit will loosen you up a little," she teased, referring to his racing stripes.

In the red light she couldn't see him blush but she caught the flicker of light in his eyes as he took in her new tunic. He shook back his shaggy black hair and leaned forward to be heard, "I don't have the equipment to do that. I like your sort-of-tunic."

Lizbet twirled for him and enjoyed the feeling of lightness as her skirt swirled up and away before brushing back down against her thighs. She leaned forward too, one hand on each side of his head against the wall. "You don't need this equipment; you just need to let go and stop thinking. Start *feeling* instead, Greg."

He wrapped his hands around her waist and nudged her backward toward the dance floor. After years of supposed dancing lessons every two weeks with her, he could do only one thing reliably well and that was bob back and forth on his feet in time to the deepest drum. And he could only do that if he concentrated. It amazed her that anyone who could run like him, with such grace and agility, couldn't hold a beat for a simple dance. Still, he enjoyed it and never failed to spend as much time with her on the floor as he could.

Lizbet did the work for both of them. He bobbed and let her bump him into whatever shape was required. When her hips seemed to roll the opposite direction of her chest, he made room for them. When she threw her head and made a weapon of her hair, he ducked and laughed. But he never let her completely go for longer than the beat of a heart. His hands always found her and kept her with him.

She didn't think he knew that she understood what he was doing. She understood he was keeping her grounded, keeping her safe. He was also keeping her from flying and if this continued beyond her time here, she would keep him from flying, too.

The hours passed much too quickly, dancing and talking with Greg. As much as she wanted to stay with Greg and let the night roll away under his protective arms, this was her last night here and she had something she needed to do before it ended. During a pause, as the drummers rolled themselves toward a new song and a new rhythm, Lizbet took him by the hand and led him back to his wallflower spot. He looked disappointed so she squeezed his hand once before letting it drop.

"I'll teach you again next time. I've got something I want to get done while I'm here." She looked around at the little clusters of people within the mass of heaving bodies. "You never get to see some of these people except here, so…" She let the sentence trail off, hoping he would take it to mean there was a friend from a far off level that she wanted to see. He didn't.

"No, you won't. You're aging out tonight," he said, his eyes hurt. "Did you think I didn't know that?"

He was right. She had assumed that he didn't know. She had never had a birthday during club night and she never mentioned it to him when one passed. Out of the corner of her eye she could see the little cluster of people she wanted. They didn't have the look of people who would leave soon so she could spare a little more time for Greg. He had always been her touchstone, the one who waited by the wall for her and relieved her incessant loneliness, if only for a few hours. She plucked his sleeve and smiled. "I just didn't want to ruin the evening," she lied.

He nodded, believing her. "Okay. But, hey, I wanted to talk to you about that. Can we?" he asked. It was hard to remember sometimes that he was two years younger than she was and had spent most of his 25 Drums time with her. His earnest expression and uncertain eyes reminded her of that. She hated to hurt him and this was going to hurt a lot.

"Not tonight."

"When, then? Will you meet me tomorrow morning, early?" he asked, determined to get an answer from her. His eyes held pleading in them and a need for her to acquiesce.

Tomorrow seemed like an unfathomable distance in the future and her future didn't match his. His future was so bright it shone like polished metal and his ticket was punched. Even if he didn't win the race and get to run outside, he was a contender. Only three won that spot each year. And she had seen him run, watched him fly the rails, barely touching the stairs and swerving around anything in his way so fast he was almost a blur. He could win. With her, he would never get the chance to reap the benefits of that winning.

"Sure. Tomorrow morning, first thing, on this landing. By the lift station?" She hated this lie.

He smiled in relief and grabbed her arms to pull her in for a hug. It wasn't the first time he had tried that but it was the first time she had let him. His embrace was a balm on her heart. She loved him and she knew that he thought he loved her. She just didn't understand why.

She pulled back and looked at the countdown clock flashing on the ceiling. She was running out of time. He saw her looking and let her go.

"Go. I'll see you tomorrow if you don't make it back before last call. But, early!" He smiled his beautiful smile and shook back that perpetually shaggy hair.

Lizbet tugged at a lock of it and said, "Early. And get a haircut, will you?"

She laughed and danced her way back into the crowd, now growing more frenetic as the night grew late and time grew short. A new song began, the drummers joined by three singers. A few of the drummers now held pieces of metal and some sort of handle that drew eerie noises from the metal as they sawed away. The drums took on a deep beat that seemed to vibrate her very heart in time to the music. *Buh – buh buh, Buh – buh buh*. The words were just what the teenaged heart desired.

Baby, I love you
Whether we go up or down
I don't need to know
We just have to go

Baby, please love me
Bring me up, bring me down
Anywhere you want to go
I'll go anywhere with you, you know

Her quarry was just where they should be. Near the stage and creating such a spectacle they actually had clear space around them. Melody, Jimmy, Sonya, Timothy and finally, Peter. In the center as always, he stood almost a head taller than everyone around him. *When would those idiots finally get sick of each other*, she wondered to herself.

She bucked up her courage and plastered a smile on her face. She danced through the groups bordering the clear space around her former friends and spun into their space as if by accident.

Melody noticed her first. Her scar always turned bright red with the heat and exertion of 25 Drums and it drew the girl's eye. Melody slapped a hand on the Jimmy's arm to get his attention and he turned to see what was so important, a spoiled boy's frown on his face at having his fun interrupted.

Lizbet gave him a sideways grin when he started at the sight of her. "Miss me, Jimmy?" she purred.

"What the fuck do you want? You know the deal. We stay away from each other." His eyes were bloodshot and his words a little slurred. This was unexpected and she considered just leaving things as they were, but only for a moment. Him—or any of them—being drunk from hooch would not improve the situation.

She turned to Peter, his armed draped over Sonya's shoulder and an unpleasant grin on his face. "Got a second, Peter?"

Before he could answer, Sonya yanked on his arm and said in a low voice, "Don't Peter." Her expression was suspicious, but also worried. Out of all of them, the loss of Sonya had been hardest. They had been inseparable until what her father had done ended their friendship.

Peter pulled his arm away and gave Sonya a little push aside. It wasn't an ungentle push, but it was clear that he meant for her to leave it. He had learned something, it seemed, about how to behave with girls. Not enough though, because his grin grew when he looked at her scar.

"You're still wearing my badge, eh?"

Lizbet tossed back her hair and stepped up to Peter. The top of her head barely reached his shoulders so she crooked a finger for him to bend down. He wagged his eyebrows over his shoulder at his friends and then did as she asked.

When they were face to face, or as close to it as they could get, she grabbed the back of his neck and pressed her forehead to his. "I know you, Peter." She looked into his eyes, now a little alarmed and repeated the words, "I *know* you, Peter. I *know* your heart. Don't let the past ruin you."

She put all of her memories and all of her pain into that look and held his neck tight. If he had tried to pull away, he would have pulled her with him her grip was so firm. She wanted him to remember and know her too.

Chapter Three – Six Years Earlier

The bazaar was crowded and home was too far to go for the bathroom. She needed to buy food for her mother and herself. There was just nothing left at home so she had to shop today. There was simply no other choice. Her mother had been crying again and couldn't get out of bed. Why hadn't she made sure to visit the bathroom before she left?

People usually sold her things and weren't unkind to her at the stalls, but there were just too many people today. There were too many looks in her direction and a few even held up their fingers to ward off bad luck or evil thoughts. She snuck down the little corridor that snaked around to the restrooms. Before she rushed in and did what she needed to do, she peeked in to be sure it was empty. She should have made sure the corridor was empty before she left the restroom but she was rushing too fast, wanting to leave before someone else came in and found her there.

It was too late to turn back when they saw her. These one-time friends and most reliable tormenters had her cornered in a dead end corridor. Her only escapes were the corridor that twisted back to the bazaar or the service door that led to a darkened path behind the bazaar and the storage rooms. They stood between her and both of those paths.

Sonya, once the best friend she had in the time before her father was caught, squealed about Other germs in the restroom. The others laughed. Jimmy poked her in the chest with his bony finger and told her to go clean it. She tried to slip past him and leave but Peter stepped in and blocked her way, looming over her like a malevolent wall of meanness.

"What's your hurry? You have another mis-recorded Other to meet somewhere? Maybe make some little baby Others?"

Lizbet gulped so loudly that they all laughed at her. It seemed to make them want to do more, made their eyes shiny and scary, the way she imagined her father's eyes were when he hurt all those women.

Peter grabbed her ear and pulled her head down sideways. "Show us what an Other looks like down there. Come on…" He reached out to grab the front of her coveralls and Lizbet went from fear to panic at the rough touch. And anger bloomed in her as well.

She dug her nails into the back of his hand and he let go with a shriek.

She backed up a few steps until her back came up against the wall. Her fingers touched the cool concrete and she knew there was no escape from whatever was coming. Once more she was trapped. But her anger had come on like a pot boiling so hard that it couldn't be contained anymore. Like the pot, her lid was about to fly off. She was almost fourteen and none of this was her doing.

"So which is it, Peter? Am I mis-recorded or am I an Other? You can't have both. If I'm mis-recorded then he wasn't my father, right? For all you know I'm your sister."

She jerked her hands in the direction of Sonya, her words coming fast and bitter now. "She could be your sister too from what I hear about your dick-happy father. Half the silo might be a mis-recorded member of your family. Making little monsters with all that mis-recorded screwing around. Maybe you'll make a nice little monster with her."

She saw the words hit home like a blow in the widening of his eyes. It filled her with a feeling so good she couldn't stop. Sonya gasped, stepped back and away, shooting a fearful look at Peter as she did. The rumors about his father were too frequent to be just rumor and everyone in that corridor knew it. "Is that why your brother died? Too much of that incest going on? Maybe it was you. You do a little incesting up on your mother and make a little monster? Have yourself a nice little dead brother-son?"

While she ranted, his expressions had gone from shocked to hurt to blank and then back to rage again as her words filled his ears with poison. What she had said was no different than the taunts they tormented her with and that made her no better than they. She had been his friend and she knew how much it hurt him to hear the rumors of his father and the sly whispers about the condition of his brother when he had been born.

She wished she could take back her words the moment the need to say them was over. By the time the need to lash out in fear and anger was gone, it was too late. Her words were horrible and almost certainly untrue, their only purpose to hurt him as much as his punches and kicks and humiliations hurt her. She clapped a hand over her mouth and felt the tears running down her cheeks.

As she dropped her hand to apologize, Peter shot forward, pulled her by the front of her coveralls and slammed her into the ground with so much force the air whooshed out of her and her head made a dull thud on the floor. His fists flew and she did all that she could to cover her head and face. She saw the wooden handle and metal nib of a shiny new pen, barely stained with ink, flash by her face and she screamed, "No!"

His fingers bit into her jaw as he pushed her face to the side and her hands could do nothing to pull it away. His hand was like a vice. She watched the pen dip toward her, keening through the hand over her mouth. The pen bit deep into her thin meat over her cheekbone, the feeling of metal on bone an unmistakable horror. As he dragged it deeply through her flesh, tearing as much as cutting, he grunted but never said a word. The screaming from the others joined hers.

She saw his hand rise covered in blood, pen still clutched in his fist, and she knew he was going to bring that down on her. She tried to push the pen away from her but all it did was score the skin of her palms and fingers as he easily avoided her. His eyes were blank and aimed at the soft flesh of her neck, the pen now poised to plunge downward. Then other hands—the hands of her tormenters—grabbed at him desperately and pulled him away. He dropped the pen and stood, back hunched and breathing heavily, staring at his bloody hand.

Lizbet felt the hot flush of flowing blood when she lifted her head. It felt like it was everywhere. Her eyes, her mouth, her ears. All filled with blood. She wiped her eyes and stood, screaming now that his hand wasn't covering her mouth. The sounds of people coming, voices raised in alarm and confusion, came from the bazaar. They would be here within seconds once they figured out which hallway the echoing screams came from.

The others were urging Peter to run, to come with them. Jimmy was already holding the service door open. Lizbet's gaze fell on the fire hose coiled on the wall between them and to the heavy fitting at the end. She stumbled toward it and in one swift move, unrolled two heavy coils and swung the fitting into Peter's stunned face. She remembered no more than the crunch of his teeth against the fitting before the darkness claimed her.

*****

It hadn't been much of a case for the silo justice system. She was the known daughter of an Other, prone to violence by virtue of the blood in her veins. Peter, the upstanding young son of the silo, was all human. His side of the story was the one they chose to believe. No witnesses contradicted him.

Too young for remediation, she was out of school and into a shadowing job where no one would have to be near her before the stitches were even removed. She was the half-Other pariah and she would be watched. And she would be alone.

Chapter Four

She let go of Peter's neck and dropped her heels to the floor. His head jerked back with the release of the pressure and he looked at her warily, eyeing her hands. She stared right back at him, with his chipped teeth and lips that seemed sewn together from the leftovers of other people. He was frightened of her.

She reached down and whipped a leather sheath from her sandal, the bright gleam of razor sharp metal glinting in the red light where the sheath had slipped down. To his credit, Peter didn't immediately run or attack. He merely waited, looking at her with something close to relief. The others made space around them, backing away or looking furtively about for a good escape. Even Sonya backed away from him.

It would be so easy. She could slip this into him in a heartbeat. No one would be able to do anything about it. She could be gone in a flash and you can't punish a splatter on the bottom of the silo floor when it came right down to it, so there was always a way to avoid being caught.

Except that they could. They might take her body outside and leave her where she couldn't rejoin the silo and be born into all the new life that came after her. And that was the whole point of getting through this life, wasn't it? To get another chance and live life without the stain of her father on her soul was all she really wanted. To be reborn, at least in part, into things that were good and loved was the point of everything she had endured. To live and die a human, not an Other.

She slipped the specially commissioned pen from its supple leather sheath. It had cost enough chits to furnish a new compartment. Some she had inherited from her mother, some of the chits were her own, but all had been gladly given over. It was shaped like a blade and made of the best steel. The metal smith has asked why she would want such a terrible design and she had told him it was an inside joke. The pen is mightier than the sword and all that. That had made him laugh.

It was as sharp as a razor, dangerous to hold, and impossible to use as it was. Peter was an artist and a very good one. Would he understand the meaning? That you can only choose one side to use? Either the nib would have to be replaced to use it as a knife or the blade removed to use it as a pen.

She held out the bladed pen on its sheath toward him, resting it on both her scarred palms. "This is for you. I just want you to understand. I'd like you to forgive me. I forgive you."

He almost bristled at those final words, but the stiffness in his posture was fleeting and he touched the blade with a careful finger. He hissed, drew back his hand and sucked on the pad of his finger. The blade was as sharp as it could be made to be. He looked at it for a few moments and then back at her, his eyes searching hers. Lizbet thought she saw understanding there and that made her glad. He gave one firm nod, took the pen by the nib and slipped it back into the sheath. He said nothing, but then she didn't expect him to. The nod was all she needed and she felt the weight she'd been carrying all this time fall off of her shoulders.

"Be well, Peter. Try to have a good life."

He would have to choose which side of the gift to use. He'd been straddling the issue for all these years, bullying and mean when it suited him and the talented artist when that suited him better. He was a lot like her father that way and they both knew that. There was nothing more to say so she simply nodded toward the others, still clustered a little away from her, and walked away.

Chapter Five

Finally, it was over. She felt surprisingly good about the whole thing as she walked and then danced her way back toward her customary spot. The lights started blinking white and red, telling everyone it was almost time to go. When she got closer, she saw Greg at his spot, though he was sitting with his back against the wall. He rubbed at the muscles in his legs, his expression conveying how sore he was from all the training he'd been doing for the race. That he had come and danced with her all evening when he probably just wanted to rest made her heart tug in her chest. She pushed the feeling away and tried to smile like nothing was wrong. At least he couldn't have seen what she did because there was no way he would be so casual if he had.

He seemed to feel the weight of her gaze and looked up, a smile replacing the look of strain. He hopped up without hesitation and met her on the dance floor in a few quick strides. They had just a few minutes before it was time to go, plenty of time for one more dance.

The music switched to a slower rhythm, like it always did for the last dance, and Greg grinned as he took her hand in his and wrapped the other around her waist. He pulled her close and she leaned her head on his shoulder. It was a perfect place to be, made even more perfect right then because she knew it would be the last time.

He must have sensed that more was going on than she was saying. When he leaned back to try to look at her face, she closed her eyes and ignored the signal. He waited a moment, sighed and then gave up, held her close and let her lead the slow dance. Too soon, the last beat of music ended and the lights came up, bright and harsh. Eyes blinked all around and illicit bottles of corn hooch were tucked away into pockets.

There was no avoiding it so she looked up at Greg and smiled. "I'm fine. It's just that I like this so much. I'm going to miss it."

He nodded, looking relieved that it wasn't something more. He stepped back from her and shoved a hand in his pocket, looking undecided for a moment. He seemed to be working up his nerve for something. "Uh, I have to ask you something," he blurted suddenly, his cheeks going pink.

A quick glance told Lizbet all she needed to know. Greg patting something in his pocket, his nervousness about asking her something and her aging out of 25 Drums where he could be sure of seeing her regularly all spoke to one thing. He was going to declare for her. That she could not let happen. This was going to be bad enough for him without that, too.

Lizbet reached out a hand quickly and tucked it under his arm, forcing him to walk with her toward the bag claim area.

She put a bright tone in her voice and said, "Tomorrow, remember. I'm so tired tonight and we've got a date for the morning if I'm not mistaken."

He nodded, swallowed loudly and walked with her to the window where they stood in line behind everyone else to get their belongings. There were ears everywhere and it wasn't going unnoticed that she was holding onto his arm. Racers were special and just holding onto him was tarnishing that specialness. She let her hand drop and hugged herself as if she were cold to cover the move.

Greg didn't notice the falseness, only that she was cold. He craned his neck to see how many people were ahead of them and looked helpless in his desire to warm her up. Other than taking off his coveralls, there wasn't much he could do.

"Don't worry, Greg. I'm fine. I just got too heated up from all the dancing. It passes quickly."

He nodded again, relief clear on his young and handsome face. "I've got a curfew," he said, looking apologetic.

"Of course! I'm so sorry I didn't think of that. I guess they keep you to a pretty tight schedule."

"You have no idea," he replied, laughing.

"Do you…?" she let the question trail off, her hand waving toward the window where her things were stored.

"No. I just came as I am."

She looked around, trying to gage how closely people were watching. It wasn't obvious, but it was there so she settled for squeezing his hand again quickly and letting it drop. "You go ahead then. I'll see you tomorrow."

As she waved at his retreating back, Lizbet tried to remember that what she was doing was better for him as well as herself. She'd tried to think of all the ways life would be alright if she stayed with Greg. There was no question that she wished she could do that. But it wouldn't be better for him and how much better would it really be for her if she eased her loneliness by isolating someone else? They could never have children. The risk of them being marginalized was too great. Even if he won the race and the privilege of making the run outside—and all that came with it—he would lose the benefits by being with her. He might get first pick of available jobs but how would they treat him knowing he was matched to her? No, this wasn't her doing but it was hers to fix, once and for all.

Chapter Six – Thirteen Years Earlier

The banging on the door frightened Lizbet. She woke crying for her mother but her mother didn't come. Instead, she heard yelling coming from the living room. It sounded like when her mother got really mad and tried to cry and yell at the same time. Usually she did that because her father had disappeared for too long again.

But it wasn't just her mom this time. There were other voices, angry voices of men she didn't know. Lizbet wiped her face on her blanket and got out of bed, tiptoeing to the door to peek into the living room.

The lights were on, even though it was long past bed time. It made her blink and rub her eyes. Her mother was standing in the middle of the room in her sleep shirt with her hair standing up every which way and yelling at some men who stood near the door. They were wearing tan coveralls and had the patch for the deputies on their pockets. Lizbet knew that patch because she was always supposed to find people wearing a patch with a star on it if she got lost or needed help. But why were they yelling at her mother? And why was she yelling at them?

No one had seen her yet so she pushed the door till it was almost closed and peeked out from the crack left to her. Whatever was going on, it was probably something her mother would get mad at her for if she saw her.

"Listen Katrina, this is not a mistake and we need to find Roger," the taller deputy said, holding his hand out like he wanted her mother to calm down.

"You're crazy! My husband did not do this! She must have fallen or something. Why are you saying Roger did this? I just don't understand," her mother screamed, her hands on her head and then out like she wanted to shove the deputies away.

The smaller deputy gestured her mother toward the couch and asked her to sit. When she didn't, he pulled her gently and she let him. She looked so confused it made Lizbet even more frightened. What had Daddy done?

"Katrina, I know this is hard and that's why we're here. To try to explain before it's all over the silo. They're looking for him right now and there are only so many places to go. We'll find him."

"But what…why…how do you know it was him? How do you know it wasn't an accident?" she asked, tears running down her cheeks. She sat down on the couch when the deputy motioned for her to, but she looked like she might jump right back up again.

The taller deputy sat down next to her mother and took her hand. He spoke quietly but not so much so that Lizbet couldn't hear what he said.

"It's not a mistake and it wasn't an accident. Someone was nearby and heard them. He didn't get a chance to throw the woman over the rail like he did the others but she was already dead. He was seen. And her hair was already cut, so we know this one is just like the others. Katrina, there are six young mothers who are dead. And now we know it was Roger. There's no mistake."

"You don't know it was him. I see people I don't know all the time," her mother argued.

"He's a porter. People know who he is. He was wearing red coveralls instead of his own, but it was him. There's no doubt. Another witness saw him running up the stairs not a minute later and confirmed who it was and the red coveralls."

Her mother sobbed and put her head in her hands, bending over and rocking back and forth while she wailed. The deputies looked at each other and one nodded toward the door.

"Katrina, we aren't sure he might not try to come back here," the taller deputy said. He said it with a low tone, gentle and calming, like he didn't want to scare her. He said it just like the medic said it wouldn't hurt right before he poked her with a needle. That just made what the deputy said scarier.

Her mother's sobs cut off in mid-hitch and her head popped up, a look of panic on her face. Lizbet squeezed the door crack a little more, trying to make herself smaller. If her mother was scared, then she should be, too.

"We need to look around and see if he left...well, evidence. I mean, he cuts their hair. We think he might keep it," the shorter deputy said and sounded sorry to have to say it.

"Oh, Silo," her mother said, all her breath coming out in a quiet whoosh.

"Just sit here and try to be calm. Jim is going to sit with you while I go look," the taller deputy said, easing himself up from the couch as if he might break it by moving too fast. Or break her mother.

Lizbet pushed the door almost completely closed as the deputy passed on his way toward her parent's bedroom, then open again when she heard him moving about in there and out of sight. Her mother was sitting now but she wasn't doing anything, just staring straight ahead with a blank look on her face. The deputy, Jim, was stroking her hand and telling her it was going to be alright.

Just then the compartment door opened and two more deputies came in, both of them red faced and sweaty. One was old and a little bit fat while the other was very young, but big and strong looking. They looked around and the fat one said, "No sign of him. We came up from the station in case he comes back here. The sheriff thinks he'll head this way eventually once he thinks it's safe. Once he thinks he got away."

Jim nodded and cut his eyes toward her mother, still sitting there blankly like she didn't even notice the new people in their compartment. The fat deputy nodded and told the young one to stand behind the door while he pulled one of their dinner chairs over and sat in a spot you couldn't see from the door if it opened.

Lizbet heard a noise from her parent's bedroom and then the taller deputy came running out into the living room with her Daddy's special box in his hand.

"I found something. It was on the dresser, right out in the open!"

Her mother finally seemed to register that something more was going on. She moved her head stiffly toward the deputy holding the box. Her face changed the moment her eyes found the box in his hands, becoming a mask of fearful anger. She pointed and yelled, "Don't touch that! No one is supposed to touch that! It's his private box. Everyone needs some privacy!"

All the deputies looked at each other, unsure what they should say to that, or so it looked to Lizbet. It was how she felt when her mother said something she couldn't figure out. Then the fat one twirled his finger in the air and said, "Open it. Where we all can see what you do and can testify to what is found."

The tall one clicked open the latch and Lizbet felt her knees shake. No one was ever, ever supposed to touch the box. She had picked it up once when her Daddy was dusting the dresser and had put it on the bed, trying to be helpful. She wasn't trying to pry but he had gotten so mad his face had turned red and his eyes changed into something scary. They had gone flat, like he didn't know her. They had almost looked like drawings of eyes rather than eyes. When she had cried, he had closed his eyes for a moment and then his face had changed back into Daddy's once again. No, no one was supposed to touch the box and certainly not open it.

The tall man leaned forward and put the box down on the table, wiping his hands off on his coveralls after he did. "Others be damned, it *was* him." He said it quietly and quickly, like he was out of breath. Lizbet wanted to cry.

Her mother leaned forward and looked into the box. Her eyes got so wide that Lizbet could see white all around and her mouth hung open. She reached out and snatched at the box, grabbed something out of it and started making terrible choking noises. Then she stood up on the couch and held her hand out, gripping whatever it was out in front of her.

The first two deputies grabbed at her mother, one of them gripping the arm that held whatever it was from the box. The fat deputy told her to drop it but it wasn't until the taller deputy squeezed her arm so hard she yelped that she opened her hand and let the contents fall. Lizbet saw little tails of hair, brightly colored ribbons holding each tail together, like someone had cut off an entire pigtail. They fluttered to the floor and everyone in the room watched them fall with strange looks on their faces. The tall deputy helped her mother back down to the couch. She didn't do anything to help him or stop him, she just let herself be moved, mumbling to herself quietly.

It was quiet like that for a long while, all of them silent and looking at the little tails of hair. When the taller deputy bent to pick them up, the youngest deputy—the one by the door—made a hissing noise and whispered, "I hear something."

They all got tense then and the air became strangely heavy and cold. Lizbet thought about running and hiding under her bed, but she couldn't tear her eyes from the crack in the door. The fat deputy grabbed up the box and the hair in two fast sweeps of his hands. He joined the young deputy behind the door, where they squeezed up against the wall. The other two moved so fast toward the hallway they were almost like cats. They stood there, just a few feet from her door, with their heads pressed toward the wall. Her mother just sat where she was, looking at the door.

Lizbet saw the door to their compartment open just the smallest bit and then her father peeked in. His face was flushed like when he came home after a long delivery far away in the silo and his eyes darted around the room. His hair was messy and his face looked like it did sometimes when he got angry over nothing, pulled tight with his lips drawn into a frown. He looked around, saw her mother on the couch and pushed open the door all the way.

"Hey, honey. Sorry I'm home so late," he said, his voice weird like it got sometimes, like he was faking being happy when he wasn't. He stepped into the compartment but saw the deputies behind the door only when he started to close it again.

He slammed the door back open, bouncing it off the young deputy, and tried to run back out into the hallway but the fat deputy dropped the box and jumped on him. They both yelled when they hit the floor hard enough to make a loud thud of noise. The other two deputies came then and jumped onto her Daddy, too, trying to keep him still while he tried to push them off.

Sometimes her Daddy scared her and sometimes she didn't understand him, but she loved him all the same. The deputies were hurting him and that wasn't right. Lizbet threw open her door and ran out to the living room, screaming for them to stop.

It worked, sort of, if only for a short second. Every head in the room turned to look at her. The fat deputy got a mad look on his face and bent down close to her father's head where it was pushed into the floor. "You have a daughter? What in silo's name is wrong with you?"

They all started moving again after that, like his angry words broke a spell. All the deputies except the young one—he was standing where he had been and holding his nose while blood came out between his fingers—pulled her father to his feet. They put metal bracelets on his wrists behind his back and jerked them so hard her father winced when they snapped on. The fat deputy grabbed a short chain between the bracelets and pulled it up, making her father come up on his toes and his arms fold like they did when he would pretend to be a chicken and chase her around the compartment.

The tall deputy started digging through her father's pockets, tossing things out and onto the floor as he finished each pocket. His chits, his kerchief, his little knife for cutting line or packing material. All of it fluttered or clinked to the floor. Then the deputy fished out another one of those little pigtails and held it up for the other deputies to see. He also pulled out her mother's favorite scarf, the one with the pretty colors her father had given her after Lizbet was born that was only for special occasions.

Lizbet was confused and she knew she was going to start crying. She didn't understand everything but these men said her Daddy had killed someone and that was bad. They were holding his arms so tight and they all looked so very angry.

The fat deputy met her eyes and he looked sad instead of mad for a moment. He said, "Katrina, take care of your daughter. She doesn't need to see this."

Lizbet held out her arms to her mother when she got up from the couch. She wanted to be held, for her mother to make it alright again. She wanted to nestle in her arms and be rocked back to sleep so that when she woke up, all this would be gone and everything would be back to normal. But her mother looked right through her like she was vapor or a ghost. Instead of coming to her, she took the two extra steps past her toward her father and jumped on him. She started screeching at him, spittle spraying out of her mouth and onto her father's face. Her father screamed in return as her nails raked deep channels down his face. Lizbet saw his face fill with red lines and blood spattered when he tried to shake her off.

The short deputy pulled her mother off but Lizbet wasn't looking anymore. She felt pee run down her legs onto the mats, making a dark puddle that spread even as she watched. She felt strange, like she was going to float away but that wasn't so bad. She decided floating was better than this.

Chapter Seven

It was warmer tucked in behind all the empty baskets at the lift post station. Her coveralls didn't do much to dampen the chill of concrete against her butt, but overall it wasn't a bad spot to wait. She needed to get up to Level 82, since that was the best place for what she had in mind, but that wasn't the direction to her quarters or the farms and there were a lot of people traveling the stairs after 25 Drums let out. Spending some time here, tucked in this dark corner, and waiting for them to clear out was fine by Lizbet.

It didn't take long. The last of the laughs and groups talking loudly cleared away in less than an hour, a final group of four getting tired of flirting with each other on the dark landing at last and saying their goodbyes. When it had been quiet for several minutes, she heard the staff turning over the facility to maintenance so the club could be remade once more for the shopping and theater it served when it wasn't a club.

After a few more long minutes, her stomach lurching as the time grew near, she eased herself out of her nest of baskets and peered down the landing to be sure it was empty. Nothing but the red lights and the deep shadows they left behind were present on the landing. She hit the stairs and took them two at a time for a few levels, working out her nervous energy. After she felt a little fatigue, she slowed down and let herself enjoy the trip, leaning out over the rails now and again to catch the upward breeze.

It smelled of everything below. The silo's breath smelled of farms, soil, animals and even a hint of oil. Most of all it smelled of life, the eternally renewing life of the silo. The silo was life itself. All within it were sheltered and renewed in some form or another when their present lives were over. In the silo, there was always another chance to live.

When Level 82 rolled into sight it surprised Lizbet. The trip, which would normally seem long, was as short as a trip down the hallway. She lit from the stairs and made directly for the lift. It was shipped for the night—this being the one night every two weeks when there was no night post—and resting on the platform in a sagging pile. The gate was closed so she eased the catch open as slowly and quietly as she could after she pushed the fabric bucket aside. One tiny squeak broke the quiet as she pulled it open but nothing happened in response and no one was around to hear it.

Lizbet walked back near the wall where there was a straight shot to the opening and stood there, her eyes closed and her thoughts moving quickly. Strangely, there were no doubts in her mind. This really was the only option left to her. Let the silo fashion her into something new, something that people didn't shun or shy away from. Something that wasn't lonely and alone. All would be well.

Lizbet shuffled forward, then ran the last few steps to the edge and launched herself through the gap in the gate. When her feet left the grate it was like the breath of the silo rising to meet her and gentle her along. It was wonderful to fly.

Chapter Eight

No one woke Greg when the call for a muster went out. The night shift just checked on him and the other two candidates and left them to sleep, reporting them safe and sound to the mustering clerk for their level. When it wasn't anyone related to anyone within the confines of the race training section, no one thought twice about discussing the news. So it was with gossipy glee that Greg heard that Lizbet was dead from the mouths of those who called her, "That Other girl."

It was only when he'd dropped his tray and grabbed a handful of coverall on one of the race workers enjoying his breakfast and a laugh over the dead Other that the other two race candidates considered Greg's entirely inappropriate friendship and stepped in to break it up. After that, well, the damage was done and he knew they would just continue to say nasty things when he was out of earshot.

Danny Piper, his trainer, knocked on his door a little while after he'd been sent there. In his hand he held a note, the word "Urgent" next to Greg's name. Danny pulled the desk chair next to the bed where Greg lay curled up on his side. For a moment he said nothing. Then he laid a gentle hand on Greg's shoulder.

"Greg, I'm so very sorry for your loss." He said it kindly, like he really meant it. Greg looked at Danny through slitted eyes, wary and prepared for the words to be followed by a punch line, but all he saw in the trainer's lined face was sympathy. He held out the letter, already opened and clearly read.

"What does it say," Greg asked instead of taking the proffered letter.

"It's from her caster, down in the farms where she worked. He says she left a note for you but he wants you to come down so he can speak with you."

It was painful to hear that. Greg turned his head into the pillow so that Danny wouldn't see him cry. He had loved her, wanted to declare for her. Now she was dead and if she had left him a note, then there was no question of it being an accident. Had she known she was going to do this when they were dancing? When she had promised to see him the next morning—this morning?

"Greg, this is very hard and I know it. There really are no words of comfort that I can give you that will take it away, but I do care and I *am* sorry this is happening to you." He paused and gave Greg's bowed shoulder a pat before settling back into the chair. "You have the day off and we'll likely cancel the morning session tomorrow so you can attend to any planting for your friend down where she worked. I'll leave the note right here."

He stood, laid the note down on Greg's desk and slipped out of the door, closing it quietly behind him. Greg wanted to wallow and simply cry for a while, but there was too much to do for Lizbet right then for him to do that. She had no family and certainly no friends other than him. He didn't even know if her caster would see to her planting since it wasn't exactly a close relationship.

It seemed like he had become suddenly old and feeble when he rose to a sitting position on his bed. His body was heavy and stiff, his mind running like sludge. Was this what grief felt like? He'd never lost anyone before. All four of his grandparents were alive, as were his aunt on one side and uncle on the other. His two sisters were well, though young and annoying, and no one he knew well had ever died that he could remember. No one he loved. If this was grief, then he had no idea how anyone survived it.

The note was short and to the point. Written in the uncertain hand of the aged, the small letters bled into the soft frayed fibers of the paper. It was just as Danny had said. Marcus, her caster, wanted him to come down without delay. He gave his home compartment information as well as his work information and relayed that it didn't matter what hour it was, Greg should find him. Under the note, Danny had left him something. Folded neatly into a square was a black kerchief, the color of mourning.

Lizbet had worked in the lowest farm level, a huge distance for Greg to go from Level 34, and it would take time. He grabbed his race coveralls and tied the black kerchief around his neck. She deserved to be mourned publicly and he wouldn't be cowed by whatever mistaken beliefs people held about her.

His expressions during the trip and his black kerchief stalled many well-wishers and race fans from the normal greetings and encouragements. He doubted any of them knew for whom he mourned. For most it wouldn't have even crossed their minds that it was Lizbet. Why would it? He kept his eyes firmly away from others and his feet moving.

At the bazaar, he stopped and went directly to the booth he needed. Given that she had fallen, he didn't know what condition Lizbet might be in, but he wanted to be sure her planting ritual went as it should. People joined the silo the same way they came into it, naked. Naked with one exception, that is. A single line of blue dye and one of green dye was marked onto the forehead before planting. It would ensure that they dreamed of the world as it should be until they were incorporated back into the life of the silo. They would be born hopeful and renewed by those dreams, no matter the form they were born into.

The two tiny packets of dye were not expensive and it was sad to see a row of them already packaged up in a small basket to the side of the color vendor's stall. Always ready for the next death, it seemed to Greg. He'd never had occasion to notice it before. The man at the stall noted his kerchief even before he stepped up and nodded toward the little basket.

During the rest of the trip down to the farms Greg was very aware of the crackling of the packets in his breast pocket. They were like a weight but they also made him feel a little relieved. Greg didn't know much about how a planting was done but it made him feel a little better to know that she would have what she needed to dream. His mind refused to think about the kind of condition Lizbet must be in. He cringed from the thought of having to see her like that. Every time the thought came, he pushed it back and thought of her smiling and dancing.

Chapter Nine

At the farms, he walked in without a clue as to how to find the Marcus that sent the letter. Greg hadn't spent much time in a farm. His choice to shadow in the clean environment of his family's food stall—tucked next to the wall on the landing where they lived—meant that his experience with farming was limited to checking for rot when a new delivery of food was made.

It was nearing the time of darkness, when the lights would dim so the plants could rest for the night, and there were fewer people about. An old man was seated in a rickety chair near one of the plots, looking lost in thought. When Greg approached, his feet making scuffing noises on the path, the man looked up, saw the racing coveralls and seemed to brace himself.

"I'm looking for a farmer named Marcus," Greg said over the noise of the fans that kept the air circulating from the farms and through the rest of the silo.

The man nodded and used his arms to brace himself on the chair as he levered himself up into a standing position. Greg watched him almost unfold himself as he did. He was a huge man, at least a head taller than Greg, even though he was bowed and a bit withered with age. His legs were probably as big around as Greg's waist and he felt like a child standing next to the giant man.

He held out a hand and said, "I'm Marcus. Thank you for coming right away." When they shook hands, Marcus' hand swallowed Greg's.

They stood there awkwardly for a moment, Greg not knowing what to say and feeling the discomfort of the man in front of him. Then Marcus finally looked him in the eye and Greg saw the sadness there but something else, too. It looked like guilt or regret, perhaps both.

"Why don't we go on back," Marcus said after that moment of silence. His quick glance around the farm led Greg to look, too. It was discreet, but obvious, that they were being observed and not all the looks were friendly ones.

Greg nodded, averting his gaze from the others among the plots. He followed the old man as he made his lumbering way through the farms. As they walked, Greg found himself breathing in the scents of the farms. It was a ripe smell in the same way the baking areas smelled grainy and full. Life seemed to percolate throughout the place and the rustling of the leaves in the wind from the ventilation satisfied some primitive part of him he hadn't known existed. It was a strange, yet entirely familiar, sort of feeling.

When they got to the rear of the section, where the hall of shadows was, the feeling faded. Here, where the single shadows lived, the doors were decorated however the occupant saw fit. No two were alike and the feeling in the hall was a little chaotic and disordered. Marcus led him to the last door in the hallway and he gripped the handle, but stopped before he opened the door. He turned to Greg and said, "This is her room. I didn't move anything but the note she left made me think you two were close. Were you?"

Greg nodded, feeling the pain in his throat from the tears he held back.

Marcus only sighed and opened the door, motioning for Greg to enter first. All he saw at first was what one might expect from any single person's room. A bed made only in the most perfunctory sense, the covers wrinkled and askew. A nightstand covered in a messy stack of books and trinkets sat next to it. A pair of green coveralls lay draped over a chair nearby.

It felt wrong to invade her space like this and he had to remind himself that it was not her space anymore. She had left it like this knowing she would not return so she must have done it for a reason. If she knew he would be sent for, then she wanted him to see this, to see her as she was. When he stepped all the way in and turned to the other side of the large room, he saw the real Lizbet.

One wall was covered almost entirely with drawings of the same thing from different perspectives. The butterflies she often spoke of were rendered in beautiful detail. In flight, resting on plants or in sequence from egg to emerging butterfly and from every possible angle, they were drawn. He drew in a sharp breath and stood there, transfixed by the wall of art.

Marcus came to stand next to him, his hands behind his back and his eyes roaming the wall. "This is one of the reasons I called you down rather than simply send you the note. I had no idea."

"You've never been in here before?" Greg asked, a little amazed. Casters were responsible for their shadows if they didn't live at home. Room inspections were a part of that, a part of helping a shadow finish learning what it was like to live on their own.

Marcus looked a little abashed and shook his head. He seemed at a loss to explain but Greg really didn't need him to. Lizbet was a person apart, not to be spoken with unless there was a need to, not to be socialized with and certainly never touched. That would have extended to her space as well.

"Well, at least you did one thing right and let me know," Greg replied, a bitter tone creeping into his voice.

Rather than answer that comment with any defense, Marcus cleared his throat and pointed to the desk. "The note she left for you is there, along with the one she left for me. You can read mine, too."

On the desk lay all the debris of a solitary life. A cup half full of tea, a little packet of half-finished cookies, blank paper and an astonishing variety of pens, nibs, brushes and writing sticks littered the surface. A single finished drawing of a butterfly sat apart. It was drawn from the side with the wings fully pulled up in preparation for something, the body curled a little forward. It somehow communicated a sense of energy and purpose without telling Greg what that purpose might be. It was so detailed he could see the tiny scale like markings on the wings.

He tore his eyes from the drawing and toward the two letters. One was open so he picked up that one.

Marcus – I think it will be you who is tasked to come here and I'm sorry about that. I hope it isn't too difficult for you. I don't care what you do with my things except that I would like for Greg, who I designate as my next of kin, to have the chance to claim what he would like.

Please don't be sad or upset about this. It wasn't your fault or anything. You were the only one who would sponsor me out of everyone in the silo and letting me help in the garden has been a gift.

Be well.
Elizabeth

He folded the letter back up and offered it to Marcus, but the old man waved it away. He picked up the other letter, the one with Greg written in perfect script on the outside of the folds, but didn't open it. Instead, he turned back to Marcus. He had so many questions and no idea where to start. It was tempting to blame this man who could have made things better for Lizbet and chose not to. The words were on his lips when he realized that Marcus was looking at the wall with tears in his eyes. He'd missed it in the dim light before but they were there.

"What are you thinking?" he asked instead.

Marcus wiped at his eyes and then sat down on the messy bed. "I knew she was going to do this a long time ago."

Greg was dumbstruck. He knew and did nothing? "Why didn't you do something?"

"Because there was nothing more that could be done. Not really." Marcus didn't meet his eyes, keeping his gaze fixed on the wall with all the beauty hung there. "I have kids, grandkids. I have a farm that my daughter and her family work on with me." He spread his hands in a helpless gesture.

He didn't have to be a family man to understand what Marcus was saying. If Marcus would have extended friendship to Lizbet without a lot of support from others doing the same, he would simply have made his own circle of people smaller as those superstitious about the Others fell away. What he sold from his little pay-plot—the plot allotted to each farmer to grow what they wanted to keep or sell—might suddenly be unsellable. It was a risk an old man with much to lose might not be willing to take.

"I can't feel guiltier about it than I already do, young man, so say what you want. I did my best for her without hurting my family." He stopped a moment and wiped at his eyes. "She was related to me, you know. Not closely, but still. There was no one left."

There was nothing to say to that. Nothing to do about what was already done. She was gone and she had made that choice for herself. If she could have just waited for one more day, he would have declared for her. No one would shun her if she was matched to a winner of the race. They would have had to accept her, would have come to love her as he did. He was sure of it.

"Where is she?"

Marcus cleared his throat again and looked down at the hands he clasped tightly in his lap. "They brought her up already. I've got her somewhere private. Uh, we should discuss this, but are you ready for that? Right this minute?"

"Waiting won't make it any easier, will it?"

"No, I suppose not," Marcus replied with a sad shake of his head. "No one is going to want to have her planted near their loved ones. If we leave it long enough someone will demand that we take her outside."

"No," Greg broke in. "No! That's not fair. She wasn't an Other so why should she be punished like one. I'll plant her myself."

Marcus held up a hand to stop the tirade, his eyes tired. "Hear me out, son. I don't want that either. I was going to suggest that we plant her tonight, during the dim time when there's no one around. I've already spoken to a friend in charge of the burial plots back there and he's willing to look aside. It won't be recorded as her." He paused, his mouth twisting a little. "It will be recorded as a dog to account for the plot."

A dog. It was almost enough to make Greg want to run around and start beating on people for being so cruel. But did it matter in the long run? She would be here, inside the silo, and eventually everyone became the same thing after planting. "Fine."

The old man seemed relieved and his frame sagged on the bed. "And then there's all this." He waved his hand toward the room filled with the remains of a life. "No one is going to want this and I can't just send it to recycling. What do I do with it?"

"None of your family needs any of it?" Greg asked, looking at the little bottles and tins filled with mysterious girl things on the dresser.

Marcus sighed and shook his head. "I don't think they would want it."

"I'll take care of it," Greg said even though he had no clue what he was going to do about any of it.

"That's good of you, son, but there's a lot of work here and it's my responsibility, too. We can do it together."

"Do you mind if I have some time here?" he asked, holding up the sealed letter she had left for him. "I'd like to just be in here for a while if I can."

Marcus slapped his knees and hoisted himself up, his knees popping alarmingly as he did. He said, "We've got a few hours before that burial area clears out completely. If you want to rest someplace other than here, the room next door is empty. It has a bed. I'll come and get you here when the time comes but I'll check there if you're not here." He pointed to the other door in the room and added, "That's her bathroom. It belongs to both rooms but it's all hers with the other room unoccupied."

He took his leave then, looking with regret at the wall of art one last time but saying nothing more. To Greg he looked worn and haggard, older than his years. Greg closed the door and felt suddenly uncomfortable all alone in the room, surrounded by Lizbet's things. He sat down at the desk and opened the letter.

Nothing is ever gone in the silo,
It merely changes form
"Nothing wasted, Nothing lost" is more than a tenet
It's a truth that also holds for souls
Not me, but of me
And next time will be better
Don't be sad. Win for me and live your dream.
I'll get to fly.

Greg folded the letter after reading it twice. Did she really think she was going to come back? That was silly superstition. He'd never heard of anyone ever actually coming back and knowing it. Most people said that parts of a person were everywhere. It was sort of like saying there was a bit of us in everything without ever knowing it.

That seemed more likely to Greg. After all, once enough years had passed, the plots were dug up and the bones ground up to be spread on the farms. What had been the person was in the soil and that soil was changed out for used up soil in one of the fallow plots, only to start that burial area all over again with the depleted soil. In a physical sense, parts of each person or animal did become other things, but not in any way that made a difference to the person.

He hoped to silo that she hadn't done this thinking she was going to come back as a person and live a whole new life. If she had been here right now he would have shaken her and tried to talk sense into her. But she wasn't and he couldn't.

Chapter Ten

When Marcus came to collect him for the burial and found him asleep in Lizbet's bed, his expression said he disapproved. Greg said nothing, just rubbed his eyes and put on his boots while Marcus waited by the door looking at what Greg had done.

Before he fell asleep, worn from grief as well as the long descent, Greg had taken down all the drawings and stacked them inside a hard edged portfolio so that he could transport them. He wasn't leaving those for anyone else. He'd gone through some of her other things, but stopped when he started uncovering personal items best not seen. She had no journal that he could locate and part of him was glad of that.

Marcus led him through the silent farms, mostly empty of people during the dim time. The night watch walked past once but Marcus told him quietly that he would stay up front for the night once he made his rounds this one time.

The smell of the burial area hit him long before they entered it. A distinctly different sort of ripeness wafted out into the farm area proper. Greg put his hand over his nose but Marcus barely seemed to register it, his breath hitching once against the odor before returning to normal.

"It's like this when there have been recent plantings. It ebbs after a while," Marcus said, noting the change in Greg's pallor.

"How can you stand it?" asked Greg through his cupped hand.

"I don't work back here but you get used to it. It's not always this bad. We've just had a few extra plantings recently. They processed some goats last week, too." They crossed the threshold and Marcus pointed him to the far end of the rows of tomato plants where the ground was clear. "We're just over there."

A man stood near an open spot on the ground, his face grim as he looked into the hole at his feet. He looked up at their approach and held up a hand. "You might want to stop there."

They did and Greg looked from the man to Marcus, confused.

"Son, she's not in good shape," the old farmer replied. His face was full of sympathy.

Greg felt the ground might rush up to meet him and he would have fallen had Marcus not been there to grab him and hold him up. He couldn't think of his Lizbet that way—broken. She was his flying girl, light as a feather and graceful as anyone who had ever lived.

"Hey, hey. Sit down right here."

The feeling passed and Greg regained his equilibrium. "No, I'm fine. It's just that it sort of became real, you know? Right this very minute." He remembered the colors, pulled the two folded packets out of his pocket and held them in his hand. "I have to do this."

Marcus nodded and patted his shoulder. "You stay here and let me see what I can do, okay?"

When Greg nodded, he strode off toward the man and the hole. He seemed to brace himself before he looked down into it and the way he looked away told Greg all he needed to know about what Lizbet looked like. He spoke with the other man for a few moments, making motions with his hands as he did. The other man eventually seemed to agree and set to work with the shovel and the pile of dirt nearby, filling in the hole.

Greg stepped forward, thinking to stop him, but Marcus stopped him by meeting him. He said, "Greg, he's just going to fill it in so that it won't be so bad. Her face isn't so bad but…"

"I'll be able to use this?" he asked, holding out the packets of dye.

Marcus' expression was grave when he answered. "Yes, but do you want to? It isn't going to be pleasant."

"I have to."

After just a few minutes of shoveling, the man motioned them over and Marcus led him to the site. Greg braced himself, thinking it wouldn't even look like Lizbet, but when he looked down, there she was. All he could see was her face, framed in loose dirt, eyes closed as if in sleep. A few grains of dark dirt had sprinkled onto her cheeks and lips but it was her. One side of her face looked sunken and almost loose but it wasn't like he had imagined. The rest of her was hidden by the dirt and he was glad that Marcus had done that for him. He looked to the digging man for permission and he nodded.

There was no silo priest to bless her with dreams and a rapid incorporation back into the silo, and Greg didn't know what they did anyway except for the tomato thing. He looked behind him, at the tall plants. The digging man seemed to know what he was after because he reached into a basket nearby and plucked up two tomatoes, handing one each to Marcus and Greg. Greg noticed he didn't take one for himself.

He got to his knees, where he might reach her face and opened the packets. He licked the tips of two fingers and dipped them into the packets, one color on each finger. He didn't know the words that were required, but he knew what he wanted to say. "I hope you're right. I'll be watching for you. Sweet dreams until that day, dreams of blue skies and green fields." He wiped the colors across her forehead where it seemed more firm, but the bones crackled under his fingers and it was only with effort that he didn't snatch his fingers back before he finished tracing the lines. He drew his fingers back slowly on purpose to show that he wasn't afraid. The lines were bold and seemed to bring a little color back to her grayish skin. She would have liked that.

A thought occurred to Greg and he dug the ring out of his pocket where he kept it always, in preparation for the day when he would have the nerve to ask. The day that should have been today. He held up the little steel band and asked the man, "Can I put this on her finger?"

The digging man thunked his shovel again into the dirt pile and shook his head. "If you did that, it would only get dug up in a few years and recycled. Why don't you keep it?"

Greg put the ring on his little finger, showing the sleeping Lizbet that he did so and hoping some part of her saw and understood.

That done, he and Marcus ate their tomatoes and let the juices and seeds run down onto the dirt that covered her. Then it was over and the digging man told them he would do the rest. Greg walked out of the farm in a daze. He would have run into walls or gotten lost had Marcus not taken his arm and led him where he needed to go.

Chapter Eleven

It took till the middle of the night shift to pack up Lizbet's belongings. Much of it Marcus thought he could manage to get to others by sending it piecemeal through the bazaar. They weren't personal things but they were useful ones, like containers and other such mundane items. Truly personal things were equally easy to decide the fates of. Her drawings were coming with Greg. Her brightest kerchief, the one she wore most often when he saw her, was coming with him as well. The hard decisions were about those things that straddled the line between personal and utilitarian.

Her coveralls were just the same as everyone else's, but her patch was surely her own. Her pens were no different than any other, but she had used them with such care on her drawings. It was the same with a hundred other things, like her little pots of colored inks stained with her fingerprints so clearly that Greg could make out their individual whorls. Her dancing clothes, her hair ties with their messy stitched edges, her bottles of scent mixed from different extracts only she knew the combinations and proportions for—all of them waited for a decision.

In the end, Greg knew he would be unable to leave anything behind if he started taking more, so he took the drawings and her pens and left all the rest behind. If he took the ink, he wouldn't use it for fear of it running out. He probably wouldn't touch it for fear of her fingerprints being smudged away. It would be the same for all the rest. She would hate that and he would be trapped by it.

Marcus seemed to understand his problem but was patient enough to let Greg figure it out for himself. When he saw Greg pull up the portfolio and clutch it to his chest, the look of regret clear upon his face, he came to stand next to him.

He put one of his huge hands on Greg's arm and said, "It's only things, son. There is no crime in leaving it to people who can use it without dwelling on who used it before."

Greg nodded, still clutching at the portfolio, his eyes roaming the rest of the room for something he might have missed. They lit upon the desk where Marcus' letter still lay and to the drawing next to it. It must have been the last one she had worked on, even after she had known. And she hadn't put it on the wall with the others, but rather left it with the letters, where it would stand apart.

He picked it up and looked at it again for some clue as to what she meant by the drawing but there was nothing. It could just as easily be any of the others save for that strange sense of motion—of being poised for something—that it imparted. It looked impatient and he wondered if it was only a drawing representing her desire to go, to fly. Blinking back tears, he tucked the drawing into the portfolio with the others, turned and left the room.

He hurried out toward the farms where the feeling of the plants in their resting state, with their green and ripe smells, eased his frantic feelings a little. Marcus joined him just a moment later, his steps heavy and slow. They stood silently for a moment, not looking at each other but instead out at the darkened farm around them.

"You should go back," Marcus said abruptly, then looked briefly at Greg's racing coveralls. "You've got a lot to do."

Greg only nodded, at a loss for words. How could he possibly go on with training now? How could he compete and laugh with his competitors and complain about the tank and the hundred other things he did as a matter of course throughout the day? How could he ever run as fast as he would need to and then smile at the end as if he were happy?

"Son," Marcus said and waited until Greg looked up at him. "She wouldn't want you to let this ruin your chances. I think she wanted this for you very much. If anything, you should let this help you to win."

He couldn't believe what Marcus was saying. Clearly, he didn't understand what this felt like. He couldn't know that part of his desire to win was so that when he declared for her, the silo would have to accept Lizbet as his mate and a human like any other.

"Before you go all up-top on me, remember how old I am. My own wife was planted back there not five years ago. I know what this feels like. But understand this, too. She did what she did for her own reasons and it was her decision to make, no matter how much we may disagree with it and wish she hadn't made it. She wanted you to be happy, to be successful and to achieve your dreams. That much I can tell from just the little she said and the note that she left. She was a good girl. How could she have wanted different?"

It was a long speech for such a man, Greg could tell that. And that he was sincere in what he said was also clear. There was nothing more to do here. And Marcus was right about Lizbet wanting him to achieve. She had been more proud than anyone when he'd told her he was competing and her face when she'd seen his coveralls the night before said it all. He smiled a little when the flash of her face as she'd seen him last night flitted across his memory.

"I'll win," Greg said and walked away.

Chapter Twelve

Numbness was the only name to give to the way he felt during the next days of training. Even so, there was only so much disengagement he could tolerate and still compete. The numbness wore away into a strange sort of single-minded dedication. He felt a bit like he was betraying her because he didn't mourn like he had on that first day, but he simply couldn't do it and, at the same time, be totally subsumed in his work. He simply put her from his mind when he stepped out of his room in the morning and allowed her back in, like a rush of cool water, when he went back in for the night. It was like she had been waiting for him when he closed the door to his room. Her smile, the feel of her skin when it was heated from dancing and way her hair smelled all came back to him.

He kept the ring on a length of strong, braided twine around his neck but only let it show and hang free in his room. It was his alone. He would share it with no one.

In the days after he returned to training, he had kept an ear open for snickers or jokes, but in the time between his leaving and returning, someone had put a clamp on that sort of talk. He had heard not a peep from anyone for any reason. His competitors and trainers treated his absence like it had not occurred, neither sympathetic nor accusing. He had simply been gone and then returned.

By the time of the route drawing, he had settled into his new life a little. His days of work were separated from the hour before sleep and his time with Lizbet's drawings and her memory. He had half expected he might feel her there but strangely, he did not. Her absence was complete.

The route they would race seemed drawn just for him and he fingered the ring on its lanyard, wondering about such a thing. It was a vertical race on levels he had run hundreds of times in his life, just two levels from his home and on the way to one of the places where he picked up goods for the family stall at least once a week. He would barely need his eyes to run the route. His feet would know the path without any help.

Though he couldn't stay at home the night before the race—it would be seen as an unfair advantage to have such comfort—he was close enough to it for the feel of it to be nearly the same. He brought one of the drawings with him, the one that had been on her desk, and he thought he was close to understanding its meaning as he readied himself the morning of the race. The butterfly was in motion, going toward something it desired. Was that the message? To go?

At the line, he couldn't hear the crowds at all and when the buzzer sounded he ran. He lost track of his competitors almost immediately and never once considered them or where they might be during the entire run. He crossed the finish line so far ahead of them he was confused for a moment, thinking he had made a mistake somewhere and missed some crucial part of the run in his fog. But he hadn't and the Mayor had thrust his arm in the air and named him the winner.

After his run outside—a dismal one that had been plagued by fierce winds and dust so thick in places he could barely distinguish where he was—he felt strangely finished. No one had even asked him what specialty he would like to shadow for, assuming that he would stay on with his family's stall. When it didn't happen after what Greg thought was an appropriate period of time, he wrote to the Race Director and asked after this part of his prize.

To say that the Director was shocked at his choice was an understatement. Why would he want to be a farmer when he would have to go to the bottom of the list for an allotment? He would be working on a farm like everyone else but he would have no bonus plot for his own use, possibly for years. He would earn no extra without that.

Greg knew all that and didn't care. He had felt something good there, something peaceful. His request that he work the lower farms, where the butterfly garden was, further baffled the Director. It was a much longer climb to visit his family from those farms. Again, Greg simply smiled and nodded.

The Director seemed to catch on to something then, his confusion clearing and a return smile coming to his thin lips. "Is this about a match? Are you going to declare for someone?"

Greg shook his head, but kept the smile. The Director didn't need to know how much those words hurt. "No, nothing like that. I just really like the butterflies and would like to get a spot where I can help tend their garden. They fly, you know. Have you ever seen them fly?"

Chapter Thirteen – Ten Years Later

Greg walked into the Memoriam and waved at the Historian shadow as he passed. She smiled and waved back, not bothering to ask if she could help him. His walks through the Memoriam, straight through to the Silo Ecology displays were well known to everyone who worked the Memoriam. He went the same way, stayed a while, then left.

This part of the Memoriam was always quiet, tucked as it was to the side with many twists and turns to isolate it from the sounds of the main room, where groups of children gathered for their guided tours and lessons. Greg entered and went to the bench, studiously avoiding looking at the walls until he sat. When he lifted his head, he saw it all at once. That was as he wanted it.

On the wall dedicated to the mystery of flight were two dozen of Lizbet's drawings. The most beautiful and detailed of the bundle he had brought were seen by the silo inhabitants each and every day. When he had brought the portfolio, clutched tightly in his arms, unsure if he could truly donate them, the Historian that had met with him had been patient and kind.

In a side room, Greg had finally opened the portfolio and then sighed in relief when the Historian's eyes filled with wonder and more than a little greed. That was how Greg knew the drawings would be safe. If a Historian looked greedy to possess something, it was because it was worth possessing forever. He had kept back only one drawing—the one from her desk—which now hung on the wall in his tiny single compartment.

Most of the drawings were archived, but not permanently. Every so often the Historians would change out some of the drawings for others, creating a new display that somehow had a different feeling to it. This one felt light and alive, full of motion.

They had no idea who drew them. The Historian had asked but Greg demurred, saying the artist was shy and no longer capable of drawing. It was true, in a way. He suspected they thought it was him but he couldn't draw a decent stick figure and had said so.

When his butt started to hurt from the hard bench, he knew it was time to go until the next month and the next visit. The farm was waiting and flying season was just beginning.

Epilogue – Race Year 89

The files on the racers were late as usual. Every year they got three new racers and every year the same paperwork had to be filled out. Why was it never ready on the first day of training? He shuffled the papers into the correct folders as he walked, mentally rearranging the entire administration of the race for some sort of efficiency. It would never happen. Things were as they were and that was that.

He heard Zara's stifled laugh as he turned into the corridor that led to the main training room and looked up to see her peering through the glass set into the door. She heard his steps and turned to him, motioning for him to hurry and join her. She peered back through as he approached and asked, "Do you think we should tell them this is a one-way mirror? You should have seen the new racer up here picking her teeth and making googly eyes at herself. You should see what they're doing now."

He could very well imagine what they might be doing. Probably touching things even though they were told not to. Every year it was the same. "I think we should tell them only when we've caught them doing something really embarrassing first." He grinned at the thought. A few years ago they had caught a couple of candidates doing something they were definitely not supposed to do. Luckily, Danny hadn't waited to see how far that would progress and had broken up the situation before either the girl or the boy had any clothes off.

Zara stepped back from the glass so Greg could take her place, smiling all the while. Greg peered through the dim glass and heard the drum. It took a second for him to parse out what he was seeing and then another to believe what he was seeing.

It was her. Lizbet. It had to be. She was wearing race clothes and her hair was straight, but it couldn't be anyone else. No one leapt like that and made it seem like flight was the natural state of a human. And that strange twirl with her toes pointed and her arms out like wings was entirely Lizbet's.

Greg made a strangled noise in his throat and pushed open the door. The folders fell from his suddenly nerveless fingers, the papers fluttering around his feet as he walked toward her. How was it possible? Lizbet had died almost 19 years ago. It would be the anniversary of her death is just two weeks.

"Lizbet," he whispered as he walked toward her.

He felt Zara's hand on his arm, her grip forceful enough to stop him in his tracks. She looked at him quizzically and asked, "Greg. What about Lizbet?"

She knew, of course. They were friends, good friends, and she was one of the few who knew of Lizbet and his connection with her. She was sympathetic, the situation too far removed from her for any hint of disapproval or questioning of Lizbet's status. Zara also knew she was dead.

Greg looked at Lizbet, her dance ended, as she pushed her hair from her face. "There."

Zara looked at Lizbet and then back at him, understanding coming into her expression. She pulled his arm again, making him face her. When he tore his eyes from Lizbet, she said, "That's not Lizbet, Greg. That's Lillian and she is a candidate. She's just an 18 year old girl."

"But," he said, extending a hand in Lizbet's direction. "That's her."

She pulled his hand down and looked quickly at Lizbet and the boy now standing behind her, both of them watching their exchange with wary eyes. Greg wished he could see her expression.

"No, Greg, she's not. Maybe she's a relative or something and she looks like her. Look at me," she demanded, so he did. "Don't scare her. Lizbet is dead. That is Lillian. Are we clear?"

Reality tumbled back to Greg and he shook his head. Of course, it couldn't be Lizbet. Zara was right. Lizbet had been dead for almost as long as she'd been alive. She'd been dead so long that Greg didn't know when he'd stopped missing her. He didn't even visit the Memoriam to see her drawings anymore, it had been so long. It must be a relative or some quirk of features. Everyone in the silo was related if you went back far enough.

"Yeah, okay. You're right. Sorry," he said lamely, embarrassed now that the moment had passed. But it was just so uncanny. "Let's get going before we scare them anymore."

He tried to sound light but Zara's eyes were still worried. She gave him a brief, tight nod and he set off across the vast training room toward the candidates. He could feel her eyes on his back as he walked and he made an effort to keep his steps casual and not too fast.

As he drew nearer, he saw her face more clearly. She had the same figure, the same general facial structure, but Zara was right in that she was a different person. Not Lizbet at all. He tried to keep his face neutral, but it was disappointment he felt. Her hair was straight and she had an atrocious cowlick on the right side of her forehead. She was very similar, but each feature was just a little off. The eyes were a little bigger and further apart, the lid creased more deeply. Her eyelids were not the almost perfectly smooth lids that Lizbet had been blessed with. Her lips were a little bigger, her cheeks more sharply defined and she was taller, too. No, it wasn't Lizbet but she could have been her sister. And the way she moved was pure Lizbet.

The racers looked nervous. The boy was holding the girl's shoulders protectively and giving Greg a look, the girl bouncing a foot on the floor. When she pushed the hair away from her face again, he saw the mark there. It was recognizable in an instant. Though brown and without detail, the birthmark on her cheek was something he had seen almost every day of his life at least once for the last nineteen years. It was the drawing from Lizbet's desk that now hung on his wall. The butterfly.

He remembered the words from her note, words that had made no sense to him at the time. *Not me, but of me.* Greg smiled.

Thank You

You have my sincerest thanks for reading my work and I sure hope you enjoyed it. If you did, please take the time to write a review. It doesn't have to be long, just a few words. Believe me when I say that each review matters in a huge way. There is no visibility without reviews. Plus, without those nice words there is no way I'd be able to force myself to muddle through and keep writing.

I love to hear from readers, even the ones who didn't like something I did. Readers do change the way I write and what you say might even impact a future character. I'm on Google+ and Facebook under Ann Christy and The Twitter as AnnChristyZ. You can reach me via email at Ann.ChristyAuthor@gmail.com. You can also give me a shout out on the series webpage: http://Silo49.blogspot.com.

The next book I'm slated to get out is called Lulu 394, a science fiction adventure that involves cloning, self-replicating machines, space travel and all sorts of goodness. If you want to keep up with my work, go to the Silo 49 website and contact me to get on the release list. No spam, just a rare heads up on a new release and any giveaways I might do.

On a more serious note, I thought of this story arc long before the most recent spate of bullying related suicides in the real world. I almost didn't finish this story because of it, but in the end, the story was what it was. Bullying is never okay and can have horrific results. Suicide is never the answer…ever.

Until next time, Ann

Printed in Great Britain
by Amazon